Kai-lan's Carnival

adapted by Alison Inches

based on the screenplay written by Sascha Paladino

illustrated by Jason Fruchter

Simon Spotlight/Nickelodeon

New York   London   Toronto   Sydney

SIMON SPOTLIGHT
An imprint of Simon & Schuster Children's Publishing Division
1230 Avenue of the Americas, New York, New York 10020
For information about special discounts for bulk purchases, please contact Simon & Schuster
Special Sales at 1-866-506-1949 or business@simonandschuster.com.
Manufactured in the United States of America
0410 LAK
First Edition 10 9 8 7 6 5 4 3 2 1
ISBN 978-1-4424-0177-8

Ni hao! I'm Kai-lan. Today Rintoo, Tolee, Hoho, and I are going to a carnival in my backyard. There will be rides, games, and lots of things to see. My favorite ride is the roller coaster.

There's YeYe! He has a game booth for the carnival. It's a Chinese number game. You have to pick a card. If the number on your card matches the one on the box, you win a prize. Do you want to play? Super!

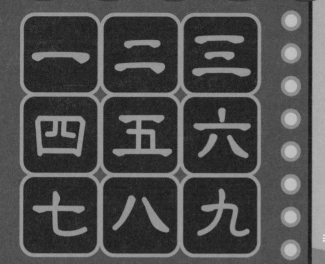

I picked the Chinese number eight. Do you want to know how to say "eight" in Chinese? You say, *"Ba!"* Can you point to the box with the same number?

You're right! *Ba!* Ooh, the prize in the box is dinosaur stickers! I love dinosaurs!

Our friend Stompy has an awesome roller coaster rocket ride! He needs our help to pull his rocket to the red flag. Do you want to know how to say "pull" in Chinese? You say, "*La!*" Say it with us as we pull! *La!* Say it louder! *LA!* We pulled the rocket to the red flag!

Stompy says we can go on his ride after he paints the rocket. What can we do while we wait for Stompy? Let's play more games!

The Ant City game looks super! To play, San San will tell us his favorite place in Ant City. Then we have to pull the rope that goes there. Hoho gets to go first, because he is the youngest. San San says to pull the rope that goes to the slide!

Let's help Hoho! Do you remember how to say "pull" in Chinese? Say it with us! *La!*

Ding! Ding! Ding! Hoho's a winner! We all win an acorn bell! *Xie xie!* Thank you, San San! This carnival is really super!

The rocket roller coaster ride still isn't ready. We can play Mr. Hoppy's hop and splash game while we wait. Mr. Hoppy says we need to hop and throw the ball to sink a lily pad.

Rintoo and Hoho hop and throw the balls! Uh-oh! The balls went a little too high. *Boing!* They bounced off the top of the booth! Now the balls are flying through the air!

Look at the balls go! They just hit a tire! And the tire hit a coconut! The coconut landed on a seesaw! And the seesaw just launched a box of beanbags into the air!

The beanbags are headed straight for Stompy's rocket!

Oh, no! Stompy's rocket got smashed to pieces! Rintoo and Hoho look really upset. I wonder why they're running away! Do you think it's because they're worried Stompy's going to be mad that they broke his rocket? I think so too!

Come on! We have to help our friends!
What can we try?
It's up to me and you!
Rintoo and Hoho need our help.
We'll figure out
what to do!

Crash!

Oh, no! On our way to help Rintoo and Hoho, we bumped into Mei Mei's dragon prizes. Now they're all over the ground! We need to say sorry to Mei Mei!

"Sorry we knocked over your dragons, Mei Mei!"

Mei Mei's not mad at us. She understands that it was an accident. Let's help Mei Mei pick up the dragons. *When you cause a problem, here's what you should do. First you say you're sorry, and then you help to fix it too!*

Rintoo and Hoho said sorry to Stompy too. They didn't mean to break his rocket. Do you think Stompy's mad at his friends? No, he's not mad. He understands it was an accident, but he feels a little sad because his rocket was broken.

Rintoo and Hoho want to help fix the rocket. We can all help! *When you cause a problem, here's what you should do. First you say you're sorry, and then you help to fix it too!*

Stompy's rocket is all fixed! YeYe, come ride with us! We have to count to three in Chinese to start the ride!

Let's say it together! *Yi! Er! San!* Super counting! Here we go! Whee!

1 2 3

Stompy has a surprise for us! He's spraying us with water! *Yay!*

That was a super ride! Did you like the carnival as much as we did? I'm glad you came with us. You really helped Rintoo and Hoho too! That makes you a great friend. You make my heart feel super happy!